KITTY is not a CAT

Hired Hound

In a rundown old mansion
perched on a hill there
lives a family of stray cats.
These cats play music,
love parties and live
without a care in the world.

One day, a small girl with two black pigtails knocks on the cats' front door. Before they know what's happened, she's moved in! The cats have a firm **NO HUMANS** policy, but the girl isn't like regular humans. She wears a bright orange costume with ears and paws and a tail, and she says

Not that the cats know what that means.

Her name is **KITTY** – they read it on her collar. It seems all Kitty wants to be is a cat. **But...**

Hired Hound

JESS BLACK

LOTHIAN
Children's Books

From bebop to K-pop, classic rock to hip hop – the cats loved playing many different types of music. Most of all, they liked to play **LOUDLY**, and that's just what they were doing one morning as Kitty showed off some dance moves to a new pet.

Dancing, she had discovered, was even more fun when you had a **TURTLE** to boogie with.

'Meow, meow, meow!' Kitty laughed, twisting, spinning and dipping along to the cats' infectious beat with her turtle.

Kitty, the cats and the turtle were having such a good time they completely forgot that not everybody appreciates musical genius. Or loud music.

A strange noise interrupted them.

GRRR!

Kitty wondered what it could be. It sounded like it was coming from next door. And everyone knew nothing good came from next door.

GRRR!
RUFF! RUFF!

The noise was getting louder. The cats put down their instruments to listen.

GRRR
RUFF
RUFF
GRRR!

‘Enemy alert!’ cried Spook, already nervous. ‘Sounds like a barking dog to me.’

Kitty quite liked dogs, but she knew the cats had a strict **NO CANINES** policy – it was even more strict than their **NO HUMANS** policy. The barking was so loud now that she thought it could only be coming from the **biggest** and **fiercest** of dogs.

So when Kitty and the cats spotted a TINY chihuahua over the hedge, Cheeta scoffed.

'That thing?

He couldn't hurt a fly!'

The barking dog might have been small, but he was very determined. That afternoon, he marched straight through the cats' front door without even knocking.

'Who does he think he is?' asked Thorn, one eyebrow raised.

‘The name’s Butcher,’ the dog declared. ‘And here’s the deal: I’ve been hired by next door to restore some peace and quiet.’

The cats said nothing.

Butcher whipped out a piece of paper. ‘Sign this contract agreeing to stay quiet and none of you will have to hear from me again.’

‘Cats don’t do deals with *dogs*,’ Cheeta said, frowning.

‘Listen, my feline friend –’ Butcher began.

Just then, King Tubby burst into the room. ‘Did someone say “deal”? I’ll handle this!’ he cried, taking the contract from Butcher. ‘Ignore Cheeta, he wouldn’t know a deal if it bit him on the tail.’

Cheeta rolled his eyes.

King Tubby glanced at the contract quickly. He cleared his throat. He turned the page upside down. 'One must check the fine print,' he said importantly.

'Well?' prompted Butcher, impatient. 'Sign there. No noise from you cats; no trouble from me.'

Before anyone else could get a word in, King Tubby marked the page with a flourish and shook paws with Butcher.

'I'll be watching and listening,' Butcher called as he let himself out.

Kitty shook her head. She had a bad feeling about this.

Cheeta wasn't going to let a dog stand in the way of the cats' music. After lunch, he and Spook played some tunes that Kitty and her turtle could bounce along to.

TWANG-A-DANG

TWANGGGG

'Maybe we should turn it down?' Spook suggested.

Before Cheeta could reply, Butcher appeared behind them – he really had been watching and listening.

'Ah, an original Fender Twin,' he said.

'You know your amplifiers,' Cheeta replied, impressed. 'This one's a collector's item.'

'Well, then, sorry in advance,' said Butcher as he picked it up.

'You wouldn't!' cried Cheeta.

But Butcher had already thrown the amplifier. It hit the ground and **smashed** to pieces. He was surprisingly strong for such a small dog.

Cheeta was speechless.

'A deal's a deal,' Butcher said simply, waving them all goodbye.

Kitty couldn't help but think things were only going to get worse.

Later in the afternoon, Kitty and her turtle were listening to Luna play the zither. Kitty had never heard anything like it before moving in with the cats. She closed her eyes and swayed slowly to the sound.

'Beautiful,' someone said.

Kitty's eyes snapped open to see Butcher holding a pair of scissors.

'It really is *such* a shame,' he continued. Then he reached over to Luna, who was still deep in her music, and cut the strings of the zither with a single **snip**.

Luna burst into tears at the sight of her broken instrument.

‘A deal’s a deal,’ was all the little dog said.

Kitty rushed to Luna’s side to comfort her friend. She was furious.

Butcher’s arrival had changed everything. A houseful of musical cats who weren’t allowed to make music? What kind of home was that?

That night, a medley of sleepy sighs and snuffles could be heard.

But a much louder noise was coming from one cat in particular.

It was Spook. He was snoring. **LOUDLY.**

His snoring was so loud it woke Kitty. She knew it wouldn't be long before Butcher heard it too, so she tiptoed as quietly as she could to Spook's room.

Kitty was just about to knock when a small pair of paws jumped on Spook's bed.

'Put a sock in it!' said Butcher. 'A deal's a deal.'

It was clear the deal wasn't just about their music – the cats had no choice but to be as quiet as possible.

The next day, Thorn, The Nazz, Last Chance and Kitty tried to cheer themselves up with cake and tea, but no amount of sweets made the silence any less miserable.

Gloomily, Last Chance dropped
a sugar cube in his tea.

Kitty knew Butcher's noise radar was
second to none. She was sure he'd notice
even this tiny sound and...

As expected, Butcher appeared. Before the others realised what was happening, he leaped straight onto the table and **cracked** it in half. Then he helped himself to a cupcake.

'Let me guess,' sighed Thorn flatly, 'a deal's a deal?'

Butcher smiled through a mouthful of cake. 'You're catching on.'

Kitty slurped her drink loudly in protest. Butcher glared at her. Though no one, not even Kitty, noticed that he didn't *stop* her.

The noise ban had reached crisis point – the silence was driving the cats crazy – so King Tubby called an emergency house meeting.

SHUSH!
SHUSH!
SHUSH!

'Don't shush me!' King Tubby retorted. 'Freedom of speech is a cat's right!'

'Being quiet was part of this deal,' Petal piped up in a whisper. 'The deal that *you* agreed to, Tubby! There's no getting out of a contract.'

'Unless...' said The Nazz.

Everyone looked at him expectantly. Kitty brightened. Could The Nazz have an answer to all this?

'Unless,' The Nazz continued, 'we find a loophole in the contract. A small mistake, something that would allow us to do the thing the contract says we can't do.'

'You mean, make noise? Play music?' asked Timmy Tom.

'EXACTLY!' cried King Tubby, as if it was his idea all along.

The Nazz sat by his piano and studied the contract late into the night, with Kitty and her turtle keeping him company. He read it forwards. He read it backwards. He even read it sideways. But he couldn't find a loophole.

As the hours went by, Kitty felt more and more sleepy. Finally, she nodded off, falling on the piano keys.

PLINK PLINK PLONK.

'Uh oh!' The Nazz froze, waiting for Butcher to appear.

No Butcher.

That was odd. The Nazz picked up Kitty's hand and played a few notes.

PLINK PLINK PLONK.

Still no Butcher!

'Hey kid!' The Nazz whispered. '*You're* the loophole!'

Kitty stirred.

'"Zero noise is to be produced *by the cats*",' The Nazz read from the contract. 'But you, Kitty, are not a cat! If I'm right, we can make as much noise as we like as long as Butcher thinks it's you making the noise. And if he does anything to stop you, he'll be breaking his own contract!'

Half asleep, Kitty purred and smiled.

The next morning was the perfect time to test The Nazz's theory. The other cats still didn't *quite* understand what a loophole was, but they were keen to try anything that might mean they could go back to being as loud and musical as they liked.

First, Kitty **CLAPPED** her hands and **SANG** at the top of her voice. Butcher came over quick as a flash, but when he saw that it was only Kitty making the noise he went away without a word.

Next, Kitty played the guitar, strumming the strings as hard as she could. Butcher bounded into the room, but he skidded to a halt when he saw Kitty.

Then, Kitty dropped the needle on a record. It was a big band number and the brass filled the room. With a smile, Cheeta turned the amplifier up to **maximum**.

'Incoming!' Spook called as he spied Butcher marching towards the house.

By the time Butcher arrived, Kitty was bashing pots and pans together in the kitchen. All he could do was scowl.

'As you were,' he muttered, and left.

The plan had worked! Kitty went wild making as much noise as she could. She beat the drums until her arms ached. She blasted the trumpet until her lips went numb. She danced with her turtle to her loudest records until her legs wobbled like jelly.

Boy, did it feel good to fill the house with noise again!

The next time Butcher dropped by the mansion, it wasn't to shush the cats, it was to say goodbye. The neighbours had dismissed him for not being able to stop the noise.

'First time I've ever been fired from a job!' he said.

Kitty smiled. She could tell Butcher didn't really mind saying goodbye to his horrible employers. She held out her hand and shook his paw.

'If you ever need help with those pesky neighbours,' he called, waving goodbye from the front gate, 'give me a call.'

Kitty could hear music coming from various parts of the house. She was about to go back inside when she heard something else – a soft sniffling coming from the other side of the hedge. It was Stanley, the neighbours' son.

‘I really loved that dog,’ Kitty heard him mumble to himself, ‘and now I’m all alone again.’

Kitty felt bad for Stanley. She knew how much she needed her friends and appreciated having them around her. It would be terrible to feel so lonely. She wondered if there was anything she could do...

Later that day, Kitty found The Nazz at his piano, making up a melody as he went along. She climbed onto the stool next to him and sat quietly.

'What's up, kid?' The Nazz asked. 'Oh, you miss that turtle. I saw you give him to Stanley.'

Kitty nodded glumly.

'I'm proud of you Kitty. You did something kind and Stanley won't feel so alone anymore.'

The Nazz's words made Kitty feel a little better.

'And you know what else?' The Nazz asked with a wink.

Kitty looked up.

'We can go back to making as much noise as we like, whenever we like!'

Kitty clapped her hands together.

The Nazz kept playing the piano and Kitty?

COLLECT THEM ALL!

A Lothian Children's Book
Published in Australia and New Zealand in 2020
by Hachette Australia
Level 17, 207 Kent Street, Sydney NSW 2000
www.hachettechildrens.com.au

10 9 8 7 6 5 4 3 2 1

Based on the television series 'Kitty Is Not a Cat'
produced by BES Animation

A catalogue record for this work is available from the National Library of Australia

ISBN 978 0 7344 1981 1

Cover and internal design by Liz Seymour
Cover and internal illustrations by BES Animation
Printed and bound in China by 1010 Printing